THIS WHERE'S WALDO? BOOK BELONGS TO:

_____

_____

HEY, WALDO FANS! FIVE INTREPID TRAVELERS ARE LOST IN EVERY SCENE! CAN YOU FIND THEM?

ODLAW   WIZARD WHITEBEARD   WENDA   WOOF   WALDO

AND IN EVERY SCENE, THE TRAVELERS HAVE EACH LOST SOMETHING PRECIOUS! CAN YOU FIND THESE ITEMS TOO?

WALDO'S KEY   WOOF'S BONE   WENDA'S CAMERA

WIZARD WHITEBEARD'S SCROLL   ODLAW'S BINOCULARS

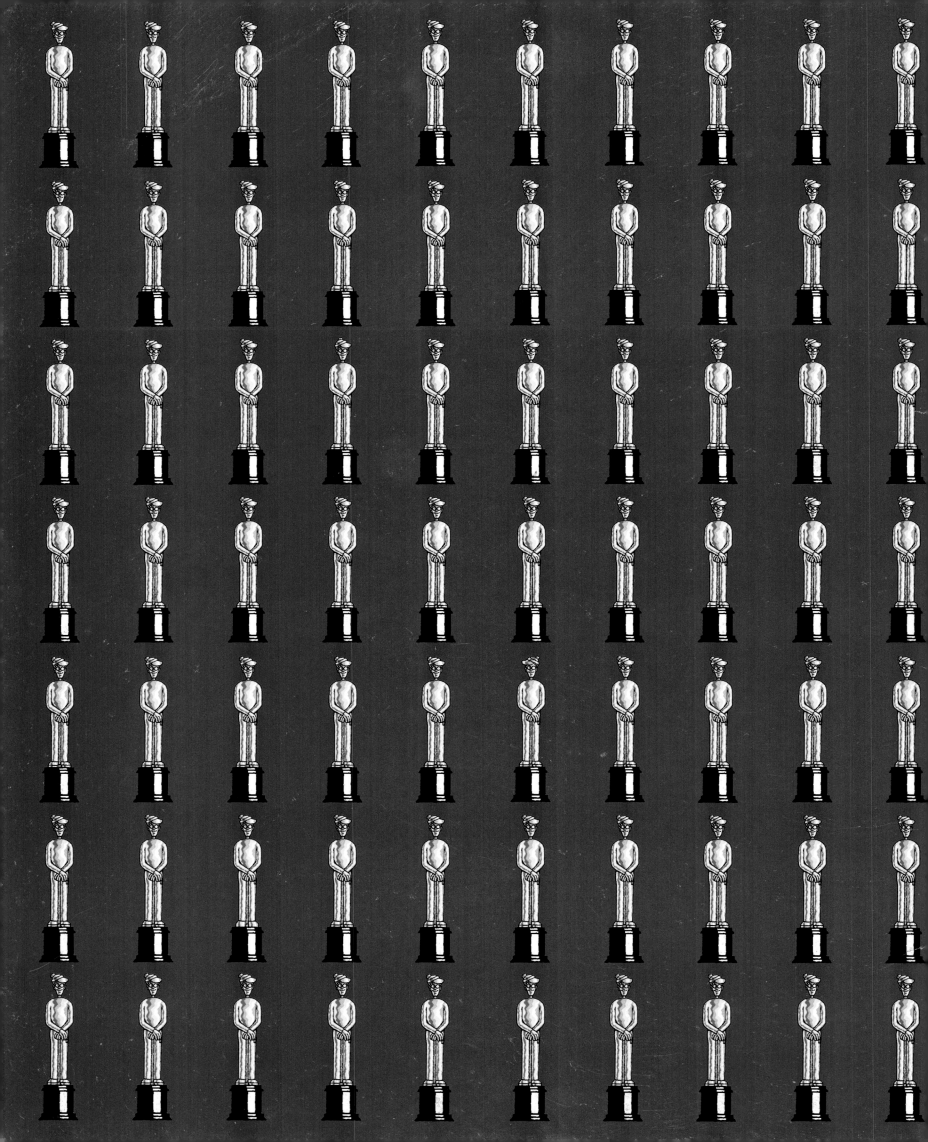

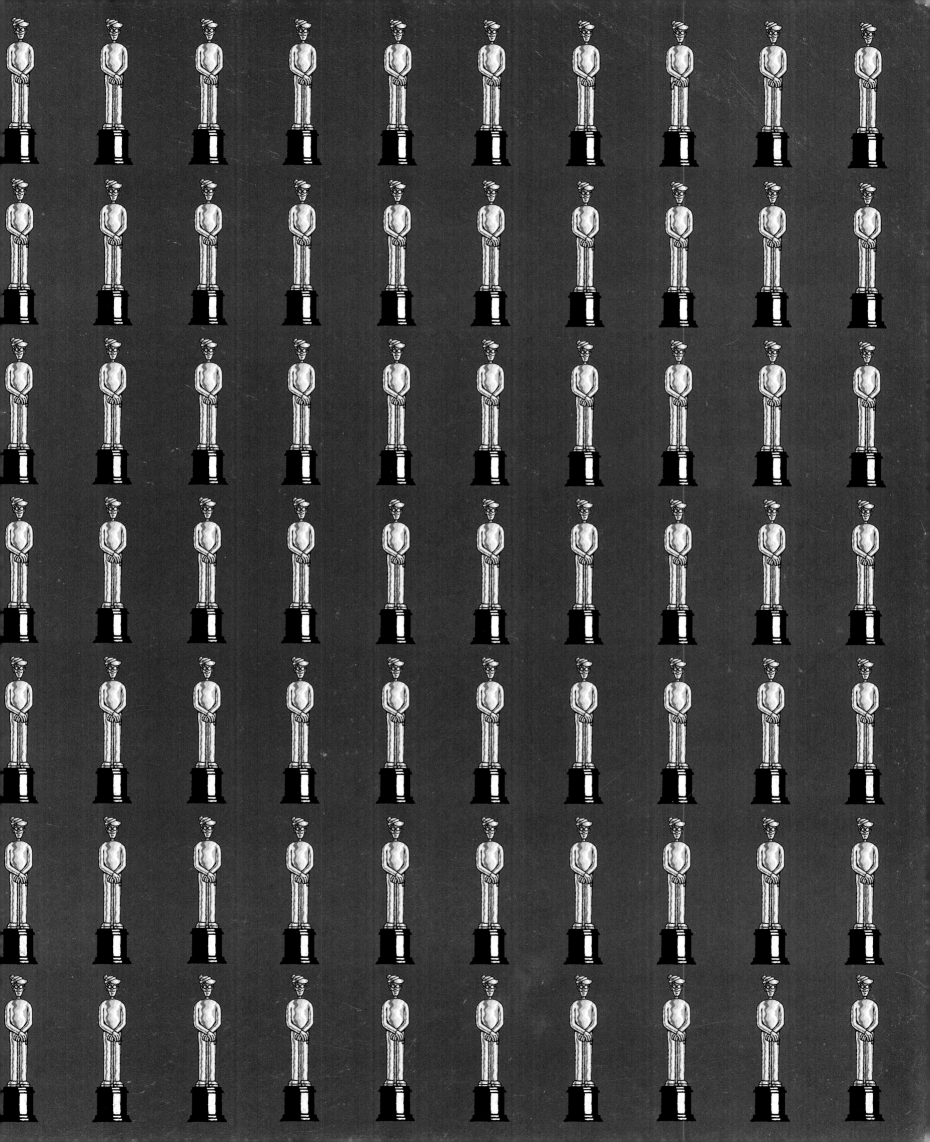

TO ELIZABETH, MIKE, STEVE, EDDY, AND TERRY
FOR ALL THEIR HELP AND ENCOURAGEMENT

First U.S. paperback edition 2007

Library of Congress Cataloging-in-Publication Data is available.

Library of Congress Catalog Card Number 91071819

ISBN 978-0-7636-4527-4 (hardcover)

ISBN 978-0-7636-3501-5 (paperback)

18 19 20 21 22 WKT 26 25 24

Printed in Shenzhen, Guangdong, China

This book was typeset in Optima and Wallyfont.
The illustrations were done in ink and watercolor or in ink and colored digitally.

Candlewick Press
99 Dover Street
Somerville, Massachusetts 02144
visit us at www.candlewick.com

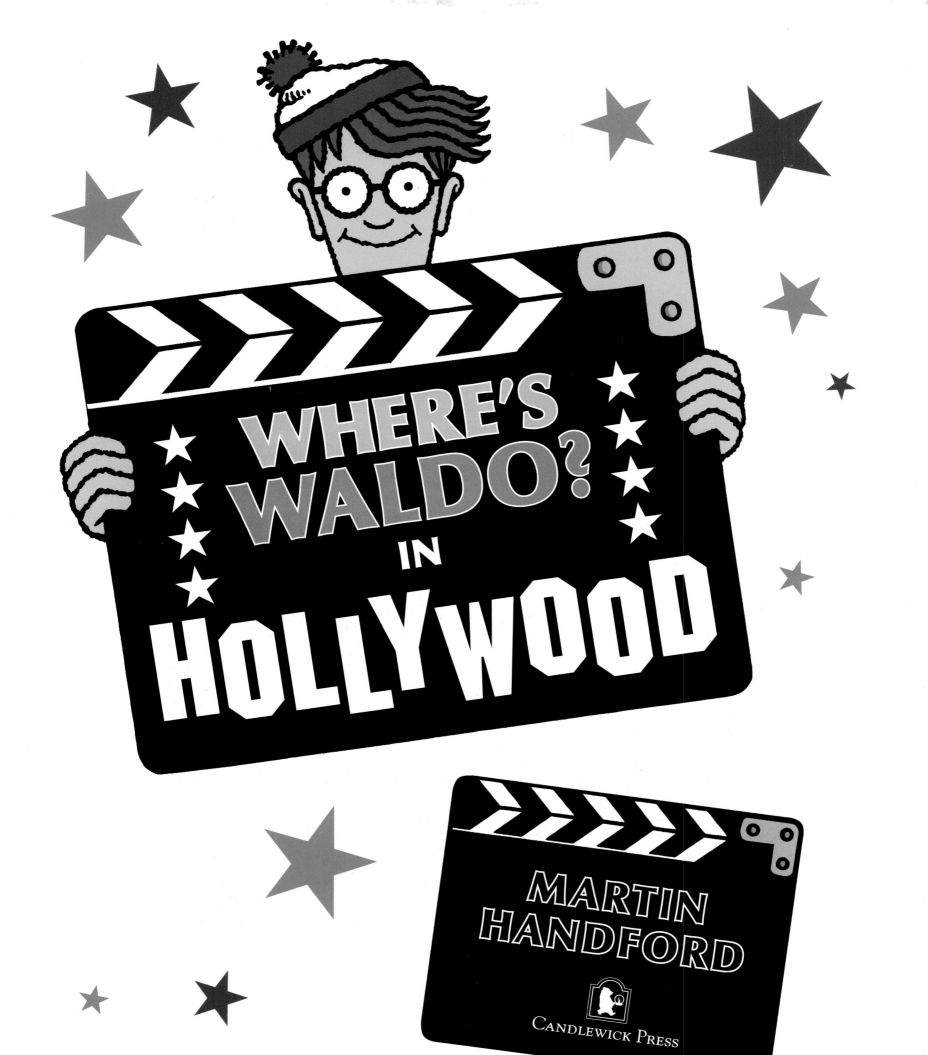

WHERE'S WALDO? IN HOLLYWOOD

MARTIN HANDFORD

CANDLEWICK PRESS

A DREAM COME TRUE

WOW, WALDO-WATCHERS, THIS IS FANTASTIC. I'M REALLY IN HOLLYWOOD! LOOK AT THE FILM PEOPLE EVERYWHERE—I WONDER WHAT MOVIES THEY'RE MAKING. THIS IS MY DREAM COME TRUE . . . TO MEET THE DIRECTORS AND ACTORS, TO WALK THROUGH THE CROWDS OF EXTRAS, TO SEE BEHIND THE SCENES! PHEW, I WONDER IF I'LL APPEAR IN A MOVIE MYSELF!

★ ★ ★ ★ WHAT TO LOOK FOR IN HOLLYWOOD! ★ ★ ★ ★

WELCOME TO TINSELTOWN, WALDO-WATCHERS! THESE ARE THE PEOPLE AND THINGS TO LOOK FOR AS YOU WALK THROUGH THE FILM SETS WITH WALDO.

★ FIRST (OF COURSE!) WHERE'S WALDO?

★ NEXT FIND WALDO'S CANINE COMPANION, WOOF—REMEMBER, ALL YOU CAN SEE IS HIS TAIL!

★ THEN FIND WALDO'S FRIEND WENDA!

★ ABRACADABRA! NOW FOCUS IN ON WIZARD WHITEBEARD!

★ BOO! HISS! HERE COMES THE BAD GUY, ODLAW!

★ NOW SPOT THESE 25 WALDO-WATCHERS, EACH OF WHOM APPEARS ONLY ONCE BEFORE THE FINAL FANTASTIC SCENE!

★ WOW! INCREDIBLE! SPOT ONE OTHER CHARACTER WHO APPEARS IN EVERY SCENE EXCEPT THE LAST!

★ ★ KEEP ON SEARCHING! THERE'S MORE TO FIND! ★ ★

ON EVERY SET, FIND WALDO'S LOST KEY!
WOOF'S LOST BONE! WENDA'S LOST CAMERA! WIZARD WHITEBEARD'S SCROLL! ODLAW'S LOST BINOCULARS! AND A MISSING CAN OF FILM!

★ ★ ★ ★ ★ ★ ★ AND MORE AND MORE! ★ ★ ★ ★ ★ ★ ★

EACH OF THE FOUR POSTERS ON THE WALL OVER THERE IS PART OF ONE OF THE FILM SETS WALDO IS ABOUT TO VISIT. ★ FIND OUT WHERE THE POSTERS CAME FROM. ★ THEN SPOT ANY DIFFERENCES BETWEEN THE POSTERS AND THE SETS.

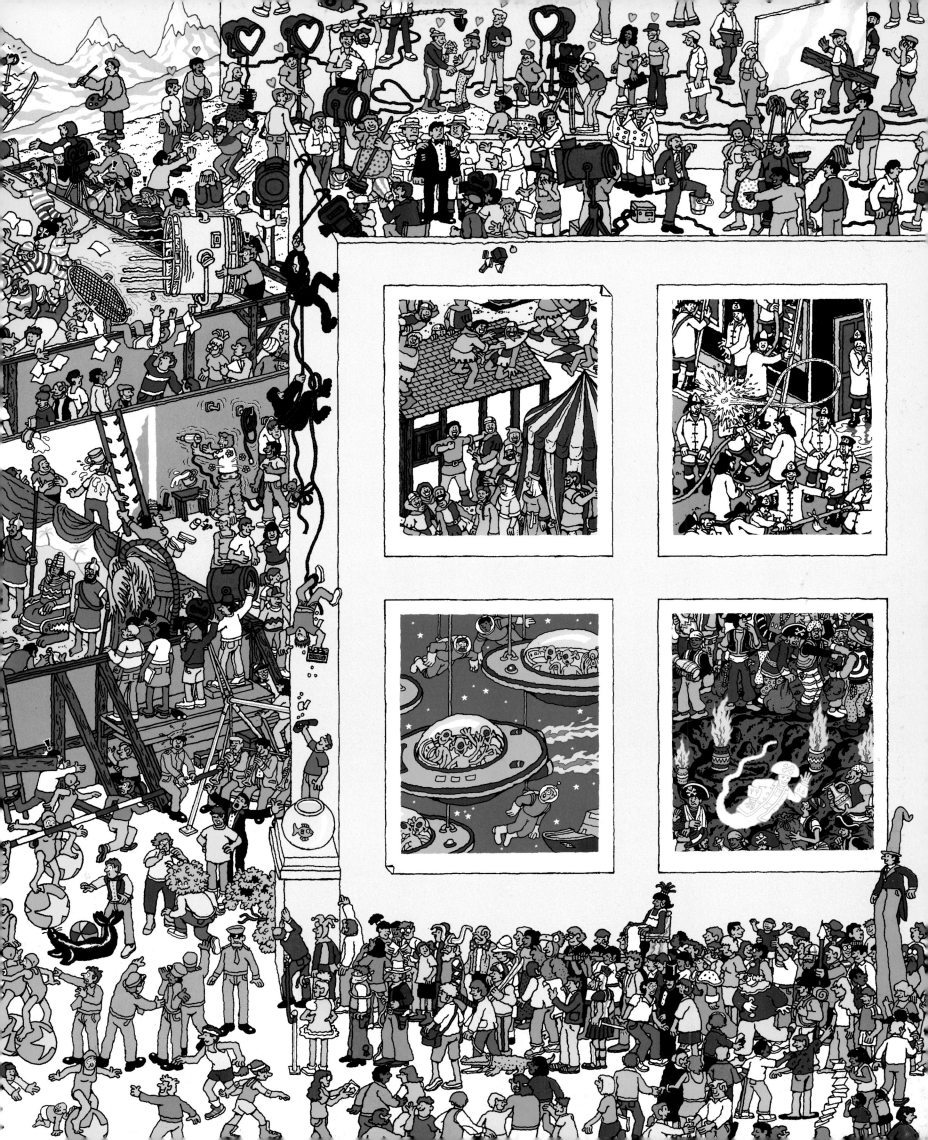

SHHH! THIS IS A SILENT MOVIE

SO THIS IS HOW THE HOLLYWOOD DREAM BEGAN—WITH SILENT MOVIES MADE IN BLACK AND WHITE. IT LOOKS CRAZY AND IT MAKES YOU LAUGH. ACTING IN SLAPSTICK COMEDIES MUST BE REALLY HARD—LOOK HOW MANY ACCIDENTS ARE HAPPENING. BUT THE GREAT THING IS THAT NONE OF THE ACTORS EVER GET HURT, HOWEVER OFTEN THEY FALL FLAT ON THEIR FACES!

FUN IN THE FOREIGN LEGION

PHEW, MOVIE FANS, DON'T GET OVERHEATED, THIS IS THE MOST SIZZLING LOCATION SO FAR! EVERYONE'S SWELTERING, FROM STARS TO SAND-SHIFTERS. SOME OF THOSE EXTRAS LOOK LIKE THEY'RE LOSING THEIR COOL—HAVE THEY FORGOTTEN THIS IS ONLY A MOVIE? PERHAPS IT'S TIME A FEW MORE OF THEM DESERTED THE DESERT AND JOINED THE RUSH FOR ICE CREAM!

A TREMENDOUS SONG AND DANCE

HAVE YOU EVER SEEN SUCH AMAZING MUSICAL MAYHEM? DEFINITELY A DEAFENING SCENE OF NOTE. THAT BATTLESHIP'S STEERING CERTAINLY NEEDS FINE-TUNING! BUT LET'S NOT MAKE TOO MUCH OF A SONG AND DANCE ABOUT IT. EVEN IF THE ENTIRE CAST IS SWEPT OFF ITS FEET, THE SHOW MUST GO ON!

CAVE OF THE PLUNDERING PIRATES

WHAT A PLETHORA OF PLUNDERING PIRATES, WALDO-WATCHERS! WHAT A CRUSH IN THE CAVE! THERE MUST BE TONS OF TREATS AND TRINKETS IN THIS TEEMING TREASURE TROVE. WITH SPOOKY SPIRITS CENTER STAGE AND PIRATICAL PILFERERS TO SPOT, THE DIRECTOR CERTAINLY HAS HIS HANDS FULL. LET'S HOPE HE HAS THE GOLDEN TOUCH! SHIVER-ME-TIMBERS, WHAT A FEARFULLY FUNNY FLICK THIS IS!

THE SWASHBUCKLING MUSKETEERS

ALL FOR ONE, ONE FOR ALL! WASN'T THAT THE MOTTO OF THE THREE MUSKETEERS? NOW, LOOK AT THIS FREE-FOR-ALL! CAN YOU SPOT OUR THREE GALLANT HEROES BATTLING WITH THE RED-COATED CARDINAL'S GUARDS? WITH ALL THIS SWASHBUCKLING ACTION GOING ON, I WONDER HOW THE CAMERAMEN CAN CAPTURE IT ALL ON FILM!

DINOSAURS, SPACEMEN, AND GHOULS

PHEW, INCREDIBLE! TIME, SPACE, AND HORROR ARE IN A MIGHTY MUDDLE HERE! WHAT COSMIC COSTUMES AND WHAT GREAT SPECIAL EFFECTS! ONE OF THOSE FLYING SAUCERS LOOKS LIKE IT'S REALLY FLYING! ARE THOSE REAL ALIENS INSIDE, NOT ACTORS AT ALL? SO WHAT'S REAL AND WHAT'S MADE UP IN FILMS LIKE THESE?

ROBIN HOOD'S MERRY MESS-UP

LOOK HOW MANY MERRY MEN HAVE LEFT SHERWOOD FOREST FOR A DAY OUT IN NOTTINGHAM CASTLE! AND WHAT A MERRY TIME THEY'RE HAVING, MESSING UP THE SHERIFF'S PARADE. WHICH ONE IS ROBIN HOOD? THE ONE WEARING A ROBIN HOOD, OF COURSE! WHEN YOU GO TO SEE THIS MOVIE, YOU'LL THINK IT'S ALL REAL. BUT THE CASTLE'S STONE WALLS ARE MADE OF WOOD!

WHEN THE STARS COME OUT

WOW, WALDO-WATCHERS, THIS IS WHAT I CALL GLAMOUR! I'M AT A MAJOR MOVIE PREMIERE. THE STARS HAVE COME TO SEE THE FILM; THE CROWDS HAVE COME TO SEE THE STARS. LOOK AT THAT PINK STRETCH LIMO— NOW, THAT'S A PERFECT CAR FOR A STAR. AND WHO'S IN THE BONE-MOBILE BEHIND? AND DOESN'T KING KONG LOOK NICER IN LIFE THAN WHEN HE'S ON THE SCREEN?

WHERE'S WALDO? THE MUSICAL

WOW, WHAT AN EXTRAVAGANZA, WALDO-WATCHERS—THIS ALL-SINGING, ALL-DANCING MOVIE IS ALL ABOUT ME AND MY FRIENDS! LOOK HOW MANY ACTORS ARE DRESSED UP AS ME! AND LOOK AT ALL THE WOOFS, WENDAS, WIZARD WHITEBEARDS, AND ODLAWS. HAVE YOU NOTICED THAT THE WARDROBE DEPARTMENT HAS MADE MISTAKES WITH SOME OF THE ACTORS' COSTUMES? BUT THAT WON'T HELP YOU FIND THE REAL ME AND MY FOUR FRIENDS IN THIS FILM! I'LL GIVE YOU SOME CLUES. I'M THE WALDO WITH SOMETHING EXTRA FOR WOOF. ALL YOU CAN SEE OF THE REAL WOOF IS HIS TAIL. THE REAL WENDA HAS A CAMERA. THE REAL WIZARD WHITEBEARD IS WEARING A HAT BENT TO THE LEFT. AND THE REAL ODLAW IS HOLDING A WALKING STICK. THERE'S JUST ONE MORE THING. I'VE BEEN FOLLOWED HERE BY ONE CHARACTER FROM EVERY SET I'VE VISITED. SO CAN YOU SPOT ALL ELEVEN OF THEM IN THIS SCENE? AND CAN YOU FIND OUT WHEN EACH CHARACTER FIRST JOINED ME AND CATCH ALL THEIR APPEARANCES THROUGHOUT MY TRAVELS?

THE FABULOUS WHERE'S WALDO? IN HOLLYWOOD checklist

Lots more things for Waldo-watchers to look for!

★ ★ ★ ★ ★ A DREAM COME TRUE ★ ★ ★ ★ ★

- A soldier capturing a sandwich
- A double agent in a spy film
- A girl in a yellow bathing cap
- Eight pieces of heart-shaped film equipment
- A green star on a yellow ball
- A wind machine blowing out of control
- A romantic scene
- Someone walking tall
- A swing band
- Three shields
- Twenty-one pirates in striped clothing
- Ten studio security guards
- Someone who has put their foot in it
- Three people with skis
- A scenic painter
- A man wearing a spotted bow tie
- A friendly pirate

★ ★ ★ SHHH! THIS IS A SILENT MOVIE ★ ★ ★

- A trail of leaking buckets
- A knotted hose
- A tug-of-war
- Some flowers being watered
- A man in plus-four trousers
- Two butterfly catchers
- Nine four-legged animals
- A runaway wheel
- Seven megaphones
- A watchtower
- Thirteen balloons
- Fifteen movie cameras
- A searchlight
- Three men slipping on some fruit
- A hose cut by an ax
- Four fire chiefs wearing flat-topped hats
- A railroad-track ladder
- Three men wearing red shirts and suspenders
- Two umbrellas

★ ★ ★ ★ HORSEPLAY IN TROY ★ ★ ★ ★

- Five blue soldiers with red-crested helmets
- Three soldiers with extra-long cloaks
- Thirteen real four-legged animals
- Three film crew members wearing sunglasses
- Five red soldiers with blue-crested helmets
- Five yellow soldiers with blue-crested helmets
- Two statues waving at each other
- A trash can
- Two soldiers with slings
- A soldier with a square shield
- Crew members surrendering
- Three Trojans drinking coffee
- Ten arrows that are stuck in shields
- One soldier wearing sandals
- Soldiers arguing about the time
- Some ancient traffic police
- Five soldiers with brooms

★ ★ ★ FUN IN THE FOREIGN LEGION ★ ★ ★

- Five men wearing undershirts and boxers
- A French flag with colors in the wrong order
- A modern airplane ruining a camera shot
- Four trees surrendering
- A rock hitting sixteen people
- Two men being shaken out of a tree
- The right costumes in the wrong colors
- A delivery of sand
- Thirteen camels
- Some date trees
- Some enemies fighting back to back
- An unpopular musician
- A man reading a book
- Three men hiding underneath animals
- An animal stepping on a man's foot
- A man surrendering to a shovel
- A horseman riding in the wrong direction

★ ★ A TREMENDOUS SONG AND DANCE ★ ★

- One dancer wearing a blue carnation
- Some tap dancers
- A grand piano
- A musician playing a double bass
- Dancers wearing top hat and tails
- Sailors saluting the ship's "N" sign
- Sailors with bell-bottom pants
- The captain's log
- A vise admiral
- A piano keyboard
- Four orange feathers
- A soldier on the wrong set
- Five real anchors
- An octopus, a shark, and a fish
- Nine mops
- Four sailors with tattoos

★ ★ CAVE OF THE PLUNDERING PIRATES ★ ★

- A man asleep in bed
- A man awake in bed
- A pirate carrying a gray treasure chest
- A pirate wearing a blue shoe and a white shoe
- A pirate wearing a red shoe and a pink shoe
- A pirate with a red star on his hat
- A pirate with jewels in his beard
- A golden bath
- A snake
- Two dogs and a horse
- A chest of drawers
- Three pirate ghosts
- A pirate barber
- Surprised miners
- Two careless carpet-carriers
- Pirates stealing camera equipment
- A pirate wearing a yellow hat

★ ★ ★ ★ THE WILD, WILD WEST ★ ★ ★ ★

- Two cowboys about to draw against each other
- Drinkers raising their glasses to a lady
- Outlaws holding up a stagecoach
- Some boisterous cowboys painting the town red
- Doc holiday
- The film wardrobe department
- Buffalo Bill
- The loan ranger
- Gamblers playing cards
- A couple of gunslingers
- Calamity Jane
- A buffalo **stamp**ede
- A spaghetti western
- A horse-drawn wagon
- Billy the kid
- Townspeople saluting General Store
- A band of outlaws
- Two cowboys shouting, "This town ain't big enough for the both of us."

★ THE SWASHBUCKLING MUSKETEERS ★

- Eleven gentlemen bowing
- Two wheelbarrows
- Twelve spouts of water
- A tear-jerking emotional scene
- A gentleman with only one glove
- Badly dressed men turned away from the dance
- Three musket tears
- One lost glove
- Four real animals
- A man wearing different-colored gloves
- A bouncer
- Three angry gardeners
- Two swordsmen "fencing"
- Three mixed-up statues
- A man having his foot tickled
- Four ladies being presented with flowers
- A hat with a striped plume

★ DINOSAURS, SPACEMEN, AND GHOULS ★

- "Hand" luggage
- A fly in saucer
- A ticklish dinosaur
- A greedy green alien
- A dozing dinosaur
- A spaceship
- Stars in a star's dressing room
- A smart-alecky dinosaur
- A planet picnic
- A game of ringtoss
- A wolfman having a howling good time
- Eight characters in craters
- A space castle
- Two people reading books
- Four cavemen going up in the world
- An astronaut without helmet, gloves, or boots
- Two bottles of ketchup

★ ★ ★ ROBIN HOOD'S MERRY MESS-UP ★ ★ ★

- Eight ladies in medieval costume
- "Little" John leading some men
- A man with a bow and arrow
- Two archers with long bows
- "Maid" Marian cleaning up
- A medieval extra with a radio
- A soldier with a large shield
- A night in armor
- Twenty-one ladders
- "Fryer" Tuck
- Sixteen flags
- A sheriff's soldier with rolled-up sleeves
- A knight with a pink plume in his helmet
- Medieval soldiers wearing the wrong pants
- A prisoner with a giant ball and chain
- Five real four-legged animals
- The Sheriff of Nottingham
- Seven helmets with animal crests

★ ★ ★ WHEN THE STARS COME OUT ★ ★ ★

- Twenty-nine lights
- Two rival news reporters
- Someone who has it all wrapped up
- A policeman wanting an autograph
- A sleepy spectator with an alarm clock
- Someone making his mark
- Six large palms
- Eleven hearts
- Three cowboys
- A bent telescope
- Someone with a bird's-eye view
- Two astronauts
- A handful of spectators
- A celebrity wearing a new dress
- An extra-long straw
- Four celebrities wearing sunglasses

★ ★ WHERE'S WALDO? THE MUSICAL ★ ★ ★

- A Waldo sweater with stripes in reverse order
- A Waldo wearing a pom-pom hat in reverse colors
- An Odlaw wearing a hat without a pom-pom
- A Waldo without any shoes
- A Waldo wearing shades
- An Odlaw without a moustache
- A Waldo sweater with extra stripes
- A Wenda without glasses
- A Waldo wearing a hat without a pom-pom
- A Waldo without pockets on his jeans
- A Wizard Whitebeard wearing glasses
- A Waldo script reading
- A sound mixer
- A haredresser
- A walking stick
- Two Wizard Whitebeards without beards
- A Waldo without glasses
- A Waldo with a beard
- A Wenda with blond hair
- A Waldo with blond hair
- A Wenda with a blue-and-white-striped umbrella
- A Wizard Whitebeard wearing a red hat
- A Woof wearing a pom-pom hat in reverse colors
- A Wenda wearing round Waldo glasses
- A Waldo tickling another Waldo
- A Woof without a pom-pom hat
- A Wenda with no pockets on her skirt
- A Waldo holding a walking stick the wrong way up
- A Woof wearing a hat without a pom-pom
- A Woof wearing shades
- A back view of a Wenda
- A Waldo in blue-and-white stripes
- A Wenda who is not wearing a pom-pom hat
- An Odlaw without shades
- A Wizard Whitebeard dancing
- A back view of a Waldo
- A Wizard Whitebeard wearing a pom-pom hat
- A Woof wearing a blue-and-white pom-pom hat
- Two Wizard Whitebeards with brown beards
- A Wenda wearing a hat without a pom-pom
- A Waldo with two pom-pom hats

★ ★ ★ ★ BACK TO THE BEGINNING ★ ★ ★ ★

Did you find Waldo, all his friends, and all the things they lost? Did you find the mystery character who appears in every scene except the last? And one more thing: Somewhere one of the Waldo-watchers lost the pom-pom from his hat. Can you spot which one, and find the pom-pom?

Don't go away! The game's not over yet! Go right back to the beginning and look closely at the golden Waldo trophies! Ten of them are different from the rest—can you tell which ones?

★ ★ ★ ★ THE FINAL FILM TEST ★ ★ ★ ★

Nearly all the faces in the sprocket holes on this and the facing page appear in color somewhere else in the book. Can you find where? But . . . ten of them do *not* appear anywhere else! Can you tell which ten? Lastly . . . some faces appear more than once in the sprocket holes. Can you see which ones and how many times each one appears?

WHERE'S WALDO?
IN
HOLLYWOOD

THE END

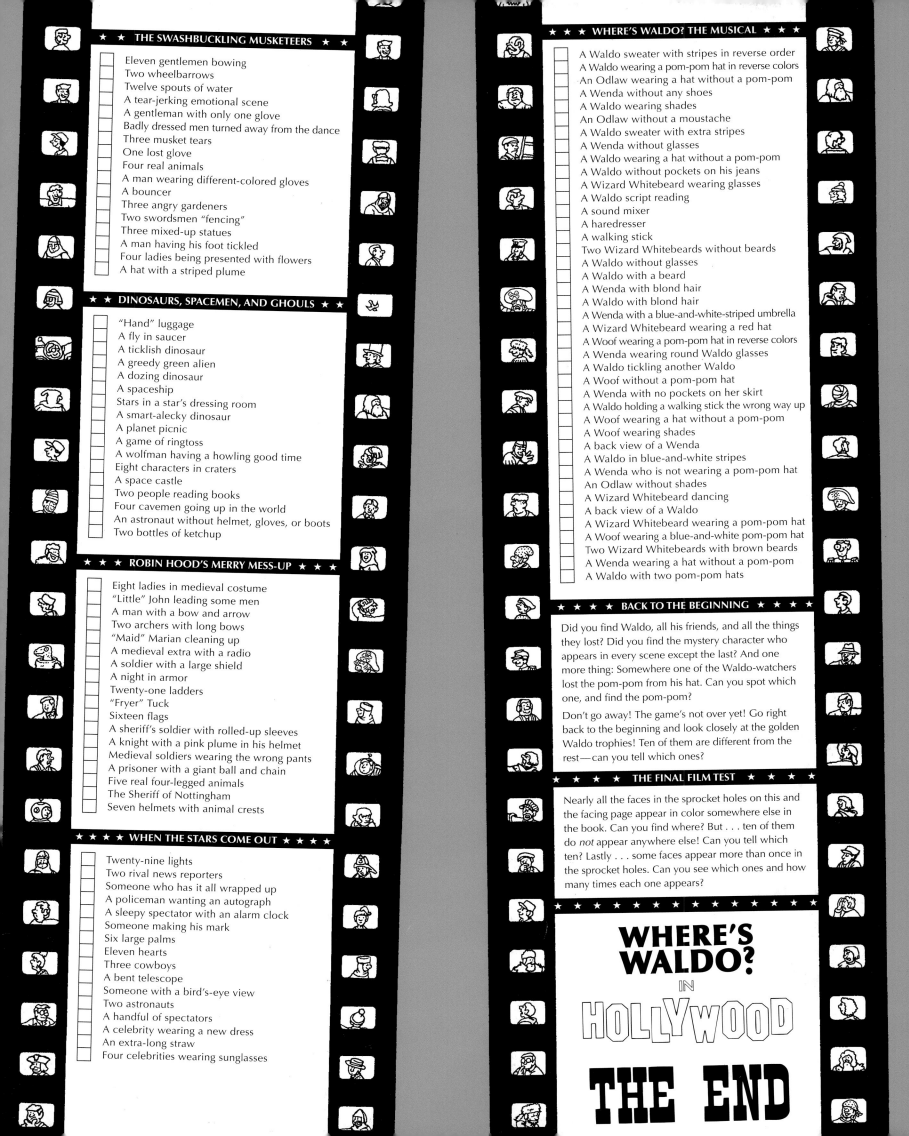